The cliff

Marie Delabos

To Françoise, to Guylène, to Marisette

X

Ten, a straight line to the sea, no obstacles, only the cliff and the sky, wet grass under my naked feet; a soft prick from the grazes of a forgotten splinter, a cat scratch, a pebble in the shoe which I left behind me, near the other one on the granite doorstep.

I always leave them there when the sole is saturated with water and the canvas becomes stiff with salt, only just made supple by the fresh water from the garden hose. Completely bleached, lost laces for a long time, they are waiting for me, dried by the wind, coming from the open sea this morning. I feel it brushing against me and seeping into the folds of my tee-shirt, blowing it up, plastering it down on my chest and sailing back to the collar, along my spine, coiling up around my neck and fiddling with my short hair tufts.

Near my shoes, there are three shells, a yellow winkle, a minor jackknife and a keyhole limpet, a piece of wood like a drawbridge and a green piece of seaweed waving all around; sitting on the minor jackknife, a one armed Playmobil scans the horizon. I didn't move it.

The sun isn't up yet, the dawn might be pink above the sea. I did not sleep, I have been waiting.

Since it was getting dark, I didn't close the shutters. I go up to the bathroom. The water seems boiling to me, I remove my foot, then I plunge into the bath again, slowly, I get into the tub without sitting down, I have been waiting, then I squat, the water was still grey. I drained it, I sat down and I filled it again. I lay down and I shut my eyes. I let my body slide down until the water covers my face. I free my hands, my head became light, I heard nothing but the sweet hiss of the water in my ears and the regular beat. Rocked by the moving wave, I was observing the many-colored spots which appear and disappear behind my eyelids, pictures, faces, flowers exploding and pain slowly growing, pressure into the temples as if my skull had tightened around my brain, warmth spread through my lungs, it turned into a burning sensation reaching my throat, I screamed, I coughed, it has taken time for me to get my breath back, the blue ceramic tiles were pitching in front of my blurred eyes. The hand held on the tub's edge, I've waited until everything turned motionless. I washed my body, I've looked at the drifting shampoo clouds which were marbling the water and the spiral forming above the plug. The skin of my finger has become wizened but black has disappeared under my nails. I filled the bath and I lit a cigarette. I have focused my attention on the rings drawn by the smoke going up to the ceiling, overrun with warm steam,

I have been waiting till the water cooled down and I got out of the tub.

I put on clean clothes, I stayed barefoot.

I lit the fire in the fireplace and I fell into the armchair, from there I could see the sky, the full moon was red, the wind had stopped blowing. I took the cat on my lap. I let myself be rocked by the undulation of flames.

I've been waiting till the last log burnt, the embers were slowly turning black, then grey, almost white.

I went to open the door of the house. The night air was damp, it smelled of earth and cut grass. I sat down on the granite step and I smoked all the cigarettes which remained in my pack.

Night has turned grey, dampness has grown, I have been cold. I stood up and I felt the weight of my legs, now stiff. It was spinning a little. I have waited until the picture stabilized. I looked at the field, right in front of me, as far as the place where the cliff is falling into the sea and I closed my eyes.

From where I am, I can't yet see the sea, but I feel it, I know that it's there. I know this landscape by heart, these rocks, the sheer ridge of chalk, the weeds. I see Simon, who is flying his kite, always too close to the rim; because it's funny, because it's a little frightening and that when the wind is blowing stronger, you have a feeling that you could suddenly fly away, just let go, break your balance, remove the force which is holding back the feet on the ground, become light, let yourself lead by the drafts, like seagulls when they are gliding above the field, this vast field, covered in daisies and dandelions, little delicate flakes. I can see the kite dancing, red, flashy, how many times collected on the neighboring roofs, a little patched up but always brave and his smile when he saw it for the first time in the shop window, between a blue dolphin and a giant turtle 100% rubber made in China, going to take some kids' shell-shaped sweets from the beach general store. At the beginning, it was as big as him, with its many-colored ribbons. When the wind was too strong, he couldn't hold it back, then he was stamping his feet until the diamond rose, the ribbons left the ground and he was running after them to catch them, to try to hold them back.

Ten, The Wheel of Fortune. Everything which is down comes back up in the end, everything which is high will fall flat on its face any day now. The never-ending movement, like this kite spinning in the sky, coiling up in an infinite spiral, till it gets stuck in the grass, among the dandelions.

This is Simon favorite card, because of the crowned lion. The first time, I told him that it wasn't a lion but a sphinx. He looked at me for a few seconds, then he replied that I had no idea what I was saying: it was a lion, but he had cut his mane because he was too hot and the matter of the blue wasn't the coldness, but that he could make himself invisible. He was hiding his wings under his red cape so as not to be spotted by his enemies and his sword was a laser saber that couldn't be focused at the risk of becoming blind. Not aware of that, the lion once ventured there and retained a pronounce squint. Those who dared make fun of his disability ended up prisoners of the wheel, condemned to hold up its movement for eternity. But the thing Simon like above all is the resemblance to his monkey Barnaby.

Barnaby the blue monkey, the toy comforter, tied up on the frame of the kite and thrown up in the space, to make him see the world from the top, because Barnaby isn't frightened of anything.

Nor is Simon. I see Simon's stubborn look when he doesn't understand.

He doesn't understand that, even if he trained for running without stopping from the fence of the field to the rim of the cliff, that even if , at school, he is the one who is running the faster, faster than Jonathan, who is taller than him, even if : "you know what? I can also jump very high!", even if the speed of the wind…and yes, I've seen the stopwatch, he has improved his feat again, and yes, Leonard of Vinci rings a bell, and Newton, you know him? "Never heard of him. But, yesterday evening, the guy in blue with his hang-glider?" Simon, that's a kite, not a hang-glider! "It's the same, but smaller."And you are small, and you are not heavy. "And the tail of the kite is used as a rudder." No, I don't think that your life jacket will come in handy, even if there's air inside.

Of course, if you smash into a seagull..."Yes, but..."No, I said no, I won't let you jump from the top of the cliff hanging on your kite. If you want to, you'll be allowed to film Barnaby."And what about tying the movie camera onto the kite?"

Staying in the air, suspended in space...An angel is going, no, that's a seagull. His shrill scream running through the air makes me jump. I find myself back sitting on the top of the wheel. The sphinx is focusing me silently. Who is turning the handle?

A tall bearded bald man in the shooting range of the 15th of August village fair. It smells of French fries and cotton candy. Simon is smiling with all the milk teeth he has left. The little pipes of white plastic that line the wheel never stop turning. Well lined up, all in the same way, they are waiting for someone to behead them. Simon stops to watch, his nose level with the counter. Near him, a man in a leather jacket with fringes under the arms is raising his Winchester. He shot his public a black look, the boy doesn't move. Simon keeps his eyes riveted on the multi-colored swirls, in the center of the wheel. Suddenly I see his face change its color, a hiccup lifts his shoulders. A lead shot gets lost in a sharp snap and brushes against the bleached wig of the doll in pink. The tall bald man is looking me up and down. Simon is staring at me. Buffalo Bill is contemplating the point of his boots; the pink pool of cotton candy is slowly soaking the buffalo leather maintained carefully by a daily shined with a soft dust cloth. Then he raises his head and looks at me with a vacant air, turns and goes away in a clanking of chains, abandoning his rifle. The tall bald man holds it out to me. I aim one by one at each head of pipe that crosses my sight. The little shells of white plastic are falling down. I slowly put back down my arm on the green velvet carpet. Simon's face has recovered its original color. He's pointing his finger at the blue stuffed monkey, next to the radio alarm clock.

Yesterday night, I put Barnaby on Simon's pillow, in its place. I switched off the light, I closed the door and I went down.

Ten, end of a cycle, I'm walking on the edge of the wheel, I keep up the movement, it smells of gas and warm rubber. Ten little milk teeth, in the box on the mantelpiece. I see the darkness, underneath, of the damp asphalt that unwind<u>s</u> and the showers of water thrown up the ditch. Ten little clever mice which had to use cunning not to be caught in the beam of light from the torch hidden under the pillow. I see the aluminum rim of the sedan launched at one hundred fifty, that's alright, there's no one. Ten birthday candles, still in the package, in the chest of drawers. I see the hand on the steering wheel and the other, on the mobile phone, I see the windshield covered with mist and the windshield wipers in its swinging movement. He has dialed the number of his home, it's ringing, she doesn't answer. He knows that she isn't asleep, she has disconnected the answering machine, she is waiting near the phone, she is counting the ringtones and she doesn't move. It's already the third time this week that she has dinner alone, opposite an empty plate, watching television. Ten coins in the moneybox, to buy a racing bike. He is even insisting, he thinks to himself it doesn't matter, anyway, she had never understood that he was working late and that he didn't like to come back directly. It was just an aperitif at the pub on the harbor. He wasn't able to know that it would miss a fourth player for the game of belote. He couldn't run off, without paying his round. Yes, okay, he could have phoned, but his mobile phone was kept in the pocket of his raincoat, put on the stool, next to the bar, at the other end of the room. When it rang, he didn't hear it, there was too much noise. Ten good marks for a picture. He doesn't really look at the road, he knows it by heart. A little further, set back from the road, on the right, there is the blue house, near to the earth path that leads to the rim of the cliff. Just a few kilometers, he knows that she is still waiting for him, even if, when he arrives, the lights will be switched off. She will have gone to bed and will pretend to sleep. He leans forward to open the glove compartment, inside there may be a cigarette pack left. Ten caramels for a porcelain big marble. I see the road in front of, glistening in the beam of light of the headlights and I make out the blue house, it is almost dark. I catch sight of a little shape which is moving on the side of the road, which is walking slowly along the ditch full of thistles. He didn't see him, the cigarettes felt out of the pack and scatter on the rubber groundsheet, in front of the passenger seat. He holds out his arm to try to pick one up. Ten finger prints stamped in the wet sand. I see the yellow oilskin and the red woolly hat getting closer, I shout his name but he doesn't hear me I shut my eyes, I fall off the wheel. I can't see anything but bright spots behind my eyelids.

The wheel is turning, like this rainbow windmill, planted in the garden. Once backwards, once right side, it hesitates, stops one second and starts up again in the other direction

I see Simon who is going round like a spinning top, arms apart, in the middle of the field, until the dizzy spell, until falling down. I would like to open my eyes, lying down on the grass, watch the passing of the clouds and see the world from the bottom up, upside down, feel myself very small and breathe in the smells of clay and cut grass, my heart beating too hard, as if it were about to explode; let myself go floating on my back, with a calm sea, the ocean noise in my ears, one starfish, a few splashes, many shrieks, water in my eyes, no way to be quiet five minutes. We have to pick up winkles in the rocks, and keyhole limpets. And besides, there is the lighthouse, I had forgotten it, keeping my promise.

The lighthouse right in front of me. Crossing the threshold, I focused the lighthouse and I closed my eyes.

The lighthouse, 365 steps, 365 days, another cycle. One step a day, one level more. And then? Then the infinite sky, the scream of the seagulls, a little dizzy spell looking downstairs, this long way...

The shore in the distance and the minuscule boats, little white wings that confuse with the crest of the waves. " Look, mum, we see the house!" small blue point lost in the field, near the rim of the cliff.

When he grows up, Simon will be a lighthouse guard, to listen to the mermaid song. He will switch on the light to guide the boats, so that it will never go dark.

I didn't hear the sirens, I didn't see the revolving light.

The beam of light of the lighthouse is sweeping across the bedroom, during the night, in a nonstop movement, like an eye that stays up. I see you, I don't see you anymore, but I'm still there. I will always be there when you wake up, in the middle of the night, right in a nightmare, sweating, because there was an earthquake, just after the raid of the dinosaurs and you have fallen down in a gulf, you didn't see the bottom. I'm there, go back to sleep. You won't fall, I will make your wings come through.

I'm not falling down yet; I thought I was, but I realize that I'm still on both feet, I'm still walking, straight ahead, with closed eyes. There is the damp grass under my naked feet, there is the wind that gets up making the trees next to the house shiver, the smell of the fire behind me, which is coming from the door left open, the scream of the seagulls above my head and the red kite that turns and spins and banks in the clear blue sky. I keep my eyes on the string, it's floating in the void, nobody is holding it any more.

VIII

I don't want to open my eyes. I am walking slowly, I know where I am going. If I open my eyes, the light will dazzle me, I'll have to stop, to wait a little and to watch. I don't want to stop, I don't want to see. What I see behind my eyelids is enough, spots of color, geometrical figures, faces like negative photos, memories in pictures. I let fly or I dismiss them, not always managing. Sometimes I focus and I show them again, always the same, until nausea.

I haven't taken my sun glasses. The tourists only are wearing them here. I don't know where they are. Simon had borrowed them for his dress of secret agent. I think that he lost a lens during the pursuit. I've never known exactly what happened. He was gone to shadow somebody about a story of smuggling of potatoes, which could have happened in a neighboring field. Unfortunately, the criminals, alarmed by the flash of the camera, would have hit back and the adventure would have turned to a battle of potatoes, until the farmer arrived, armed with his shotgun loaded with rock salt. He got himself out of it well. One of his friends, reached in the bottom, couldn't sit down for several days. He had become the hero of the group proudly showing his war wounds in the changing-room of the soccer pitch.

My eyes are stinging, I've been inside for such a long time in electric light, using candlelight sometimes, when the storm has caused a power cut or in front of the fire for hours, watching the flames, until I cannot bear the heat anymore.

"Do you think that, if you are watching the fire a very long time, without moving, standing very near, even when the tears are beginning to come, even when it burns so hard that you have to shut your eyes, do you think that you can go blind?"

I didn't go there, I haven't wanted to see this fire, I have stayed outside, sitting on the side of a path.

A log collapsed and made me jump, a spark landed on the wooden floor, creating a little black circle. The cat meowed angrily and showed his claws for a few seconds, before going back to sleep with one eye closed. I didn't move.

Even when smoke has invaded the room, I didn't open the windows. The chimney doesn't draw very well, there is still a nest in the air duct. I coughed,

I cried, I put out the fire. I still can smell the odor on my clothes.

Like on the day after the St John's fire, hubbub of voices and laughs, waltz of the many colored dresses, bangers are snapping, the accordion is shouting itself hoarse. Simon wanted to jump above the embers, like the men.

A tall well-built man caught him in his arms, took a run up, my scream disappeared in my son's laugh. They came back to me staggering a bit, panting, a smiling from ear to ear. When I brought him back, he fell asleep in my arms, the last notes were fading in the night, around us the couples were going away towards the beach.

Nine, The Hermit, according to Simon, is a very powerful knight of science fiction who is pretending to be old and weak to slip past his enemies. The old man is walking backwards, one hand draped on his stick, lighting himself with a lantern. He doesn't light himself but the covered way.

I've no lantern but the bulb of my super 8 projector that eventually blew ending up working non stop.

I showed myself again all the films of Simon, from his birth to his first outing on a bike, all the birthdays, Christmas and carnivals...they are mute films but it didn't matter , the words, I knew them by heart. Only the breath of the wind, the sound of the sea and the purring of the projector.

When I'm not watching the films, I am closing my eyes and he is there, he's smiling at me, with his hair in his eyes, his tee shirt of Superman and his sneakers that are making him run faster.

A thousand times I fell asleep dressed, the light switched on. A thousand times I woke up jumping because I thought I had heard a scream in the middle of the night. A thousand times I went upstairs to his room and every time I found myself back face to face with Barnaby the blue monkey, sitting enthroned on the pillow of his unmade bed. Last time I focused the eyes of turquoise blue plastic of the stuffed animal. His long nylon eyelashes remained still and his mouth with thin lips, red painted, were still showed the same mocking smile. I looked away and I leaned forward to switch off the bedside lamp, suddenly I looked at him again, I was sure that he had winked at me. At the same time something moved under the bed, I jumped, my foot getting caught in the wire of the lamp and I found myself back on my knees on the carpet. Coming out of his hiding-place, the cat scratched my face, before going of the room in a furious meowing. The lamp had been broken falling down but I still could see Barnaby's smile in the ray of light that came from the hall.

I hid his head under the pillow, I hid under the duvet and I closed my eyes, waiting for sleep to come back. When I woke up it was light, standing up I saw the drops of blood on the pillow, I touched my cheek, it was stinging a little.

Since then, I haven't come back to sleep in his room.

I put my hand on my cheek, it is cold and damp. The wind is making my eyes cry. I follow with my finger the two little strokes a bit in relief and I go down to my neck. I feel the regular stitches of damp wool, the double turn round my throat. I loosen it and uncoil it, I let the scarf slide down my hand without stopping.

Once, around five, there was the noise of the school bus's engine, which was slowing down at the end of the path, behind the house. I ran in the kitchen to catch sight of it, I saw the driver getting out, a plastic bag in his hand.

He has gone round and knocked at the door, I didn't move. He waited for five minutes, then I saw him go away, without his plastic bag. I have waited till the bus moved off again and I went to open the door. The bag was there, on the step of stone, I opened it and I looked inside it, there was a blue scarf, I took it out of the bag. In the end, next to the fringes, there was a white and red label, hand sewn, with the name of Simon embroidered on it. The days after, the school bus didn't stop.

I have disconnected the phone, I have taken down the mirrors, I let the mail pile up in the mail box, at the end of the path. I have put away all the knives of the house in the same drawer, next to the birthday candles. Every time I used them, I cut my fingers. I locked it,

I don't know where I put the key anymore. It may have stayed on the table, with the house key.

The house found by Simon, during an expedition of "pirates of the Caribbean" with his friend Jonathan. After, they have gone back several time, it has became their den, their secret hiding- place.

An old fisherman's house, wooden, near the cliff. It was deserted since the death of its owner, whose name was Martin.

Martin was old, he didn't go outside a lot, except to go down as far as the rim of the cliff.

He would sit there and would stay for hours, contemplating the ocean, insulting the seagulls when he had drunk a little too much.

The only one who would come from time to time to see him was Josephine, a neighbor, a former love of his youth, a memory of the St John's ball. Martin liked her because she didn't speak a lot. They would spend a few hours together, looking at old photos or playing belote, betting beans. Sometimes, after the third whisky, Martin would get out the accordion. Josephine would sing, she made her petticoats swirl before falling beside him, in the armchair next to the fireplace.

Nobody knew exactly how he died. According to Simon, Martin was fed up , he felt that the end was coming; then like the Indian chiefs, or like the elephants, he went outside of his hut and walked as far as the rim of the cliff, he jumped and suddenly, wings came through to himself, he was turned into a seagull.

Sometimes he thought he recognized him when he saw one, perched on a rock, the eyes focused on the sea.

When we have moved on, Josephine told me that she had found Martin one morning, lying down, dead, on the path between the house and the rim of the cliff. I've never told Simon.

We film the seagulls together, with the super 8 camera, when they are gliding above the field. Now and then, we only see the sky and a piece of wing, down, on the right, a very blurred beak that is going, very experimental.

I am showing them on the ceiling, on the walls, they are invading the room and I am hearing his laugh. I don't see anything, where are they? Once the film burned during the screening, the eye of the seagull, has grown until turns into a big black hole. One seagull damned! It doesn't matter, there is a million left.

I hear them turning above my head and I see them. I know that Martin is there, a little further, on his rock. Near him, there is another one, smaller, which has something hanging in his beak, it seems to be a string. I'm walking faster, I begin to run, but when I come up, they fly away; I call them, but my cries get lost in the wind.

I see them going away to the open sea and disappear. I'm looking   the rock, there is a yellow oilskin covered in mud and a red woolly hat on it.

I must have fallen down in the stinging nettles, my hands are burning. My elbow hit the rock, the pain is hurting me, for a few seconds I can't move my arm anymore. Under my hands, I feel the cold and wet of the dewy surface of the stone, I follow all the bumps hollowed out by the sea spray. I have a taste of blood in my mouth, I must have bitten my tongue falling down. I open my eyes, there is nothing on the rock. Nothing but a little lichen and a snail nested in a hollow. I spit a bit of pink saliva in the stinging nettles and I dry my lips with the back of my hand. I stand up, I close my eyes and I start walking again.

VIII

Eight, my steps are regular, I am advancing like a sleep-walker balancing on an invisible thread, an angel's hair. It turned so thin that I am the only one to see it, taut between where I come from and where I go.

One night, I had a dream; I was woken up by an itching, something was scratching me from inside, behind the navel, I was scratching myself but it wasn't stopping, the more I was scratching, the more the itching was intensifying. I switched on the light and I leant forward to see what was happening. Inside my navel, there was a knot, not the knot of my skin but one of white translucent thread, a bit pinkish, Chinese noodle thick. I was trying to untie it, scratching again and a tip was coming out, a little end that was hanging on. When I was trying to catch him to pull it, it slipped out of my hands, and began to wave like a charmed snake, it was both growing and thickening, dividing, curling until it turned into a thick rope. Its dance was accelerating, it had started coiling up my body, coming back along my chest forming a spiral whose rings were tightening more and more. In a few seconds it reached my neck, my breath was becoming hard, I wanted to scream but no sound was coming from my mouth, I couldn't move my arms, I was feeling coldness growing in my hands, I was trying to stand up but I couldn't manage to. I was looking around the bedroom in the half-light, only lightened by the bedside lamp, the bed I am lying on. On the bedside table, there is an apple cut in two on a plate near a kitchen knife. I managed to take the knife, rolling on my side. As soon as I was holding it in my hand, the warmness came back, I was regaining my strength and I succeeded in moving my arm. I was trying to cut my bonds but, with the knife's stabs, my body was hurting, blood was starting to gush out, I didn't see anything more.

I really woke up this time, I've seen the unmade bed, the duvet on the ground next to the bedside lamp, now switched off, the glass of the lampshade shattered on the wooden floor, a book open up side down in the middle of the scattered Tarots. The water from the knocked over glass had made the ink leak onto the page of my notebook, I was gripping a pen in my hand.

Eight, the impassive Justice is sounding out the abysses with his fixed eyes, a sword in the right hand and scales in the left one. The just place, the right way.

The archetype of feminine perfection. From one of the scales, is hanging a black thread fish hook shaped, like a cut umbilical cord, like a scar that is standing out against the red of her dress, at stomach level.

If you cut one loop of the eight, it turns into & which opens up and then links back together, if you lay it down, it joins infinity.

You can't see Justice's feet, they are hidden behind her dress tails. Nor can I see mine but I am feeling them. They are soaked, like the end of my jeans that are flapping against my ankles, I feel the sting of the stinging nettles like points of pins and pain which is hurting going up in the leg, I don't stop, I feel the warm and soft hearth on the edge of a mole hole, I nearly turn my toes upside down, I jump out of the way and I regain my balance, I don't stop. I smell the odor of the manure from the farmer's field, a little further, carried by the wind coming from the sea. I hear the noise of tractor engine that is starting, at the other end, he can't see me, he is too far away. I hear the phone ringing behind me, it comes from the house, I remember that I connected it again before going out. I stop, I listen, it still ringing, twice, three times, four times, I stay there, without moving. Nothing more, I start walking again.

When I hung up after the hospital call, I didn't want to believe it. He was not there, he couldn't be there, lying on a stretcher, under a photo of the Alps untitled "the mountain is springing up again with the first ray of sunshine", in this odor of medicines and disinfectant.

Simon was obviously here, hidden somewhere, in the house or in the garden. He would have discovered a new great hidden place where I would never find him.

So great this new hidden place that I had looked for him for one hour. In the beginning I was laughing, I was taking my time, I was stopping to listen, I was only hearing the breath of the wind through the bushes, a light crackle in the twigs, a hare suddenly appeared out of his burrow, the cat that is pursuing him, a shutter which is banging. Someone was shouting in the distance, I didn't recognize his voice, I had begun to call him, a cloud was going in front of the sun, casting a big shadow on the field. I walked faster, I wasn't laughing anymore. There was still the barn at the end of the field but I had forbidden him to play there, a part of the roof had been blown off during the last storm, it was raining inside and the beams eaten into by termites and iodine were looking like they would collapse.

That's where I found him, in the hay, a little stunned but unscathed, in the middle of a mass of rotten beams. I took him all the same to the hospital, he was fine but he insisted on having a plaster, it would be more credible when he tells the story to Melanie.

It wasn't the first time. "The new great hidden place" was just adding to the list of his exploits, a few lines under "The striking drawers", when he had jumped from the top of the bunk beds for his tests for kite flying. The operation had supposedly been adjusted in an accurate way, to land on the cushions to pile up onto the wooden floor. But the drawers? Yes, I was absolutely sure I hadn't moved them to vacuum the room. A few stitches, a plaster and I was taking him back home.

He couldn't be there. I looked for him everywhere, I called him, I shouted his name that resonated against the walls of the empty house, I ran across the field until the rim of the cliff, I called again and again, my voice was lost between the sound of the waves and the screams of the seagulls.

I collapsed on the grass and I stayed there, focusing on the horizon, without moving, staring into space, until the wind get up and the rain begin to fall, until I felt the mud forming under my knees.

I went to the hospital. There was no photo of the Alps, just a young man in white coat who explained to me with simple words that he hadn't suffered.

I didn't say anything. He was trying to withstand my stare but his, a little too bright, were looking from the wall to the blue linoleum floor, then were going up to focus on the bulletin board, behind me. His dark tortoiseshell glasses and his three days growth of beard are not enough to make him seem more than twenty five. Maybe it was the first time. I had seen him, when I arrived, talking with another person behind the plate glass window of the office. He must have pushed his glasses up at least five times with his finger during the conversation, then he was gone outside to smoke a cigarette before coming to meet me. My eyes fell on the bright metal of his brand new stethoscope, for a moment I saw myself tightening the black rubber gut around his neck.

I held out my hand to him, he stepped back and let go of the forms he was holding in his hand. The white slips scattered on the ground. I squatted with him to pick them up. Standing up, I shook his hand, I said thank you to him and I went away.

I know that Simon was frightened. I know that he has been left on his own in the dark and that he was cold. He must have tried to call me, I didn't hear him, I wasn't there, I didn't feel the coldness.

When I came back home, he wasn't there. I thought that he had gone to play outside, his schoolbag was not there, I haven't seen it. I had put the envelope on the table, with the key and the bread. I was nervous, quite pleased that he didn't came back straightaway, I wasn't worrying. He knew the bus driver who was dropping him off five minutes'walk from the house, he knew about that I wasn't going to get him, I had an appointment in town. It had gone dark, he still wasn't there, I called Jonathan's mother, she hadn't seen him. Jonathan was ill, he hadn't gone to school, Simon must have come back alone. I went out into the field, I called, no answer, then the phone rang.

In the secretarial offices, they have given me back Simon's clothes, they had rinsed the oilskin, I roll it into a bowl around the sneakers covered in mud.

There was this man, in the waiting room, in dark suit, sat on a chair, between two policemen, his head in his hands. He was pressing a white bloody handkerchief on his forehead. When I went in front of him, he raised his haggard face to me, he tried to say something but no word came out of his mouth. I looked away and went out running.

A few days later, I brought Simon back home, in a metal box. It wasn't really Simon, just his body, reduced to ashes. There hasn't been ceremony. I never go to the cemetery.

I brought the urn back home and I put it next to the fire place, I watched the flames reflecting on the cold metal, warming it.

I sat down near it and I closed my eyes, I saw his cheeks go red as a result of sitting and looking at the fire.

That night I slept in his bed with his monkey Barnaby, in the sheets still keeping his smell, to see what he was seeing. What he saw that morning, before going to school.

Simon won't come back, he will never be ten years old, he won't know teenage acne and will never tell me "in any case, you don't understand."

I am feeling the void inside, I am feeling the cold urn against my stomach, I am feeling the weight of the card game in my pocket and I am still walking to the rim of the cliff.

VII

Seven, one day my prince will come, and he will take me to Italy in his red convertible.

Girl stories according to Simon, in spite of that he had, put up on the wall of his bedroom next to his bed, a drawing covered of hearts of all colors, signed Melanie, the nicest in the class.

Melanie often came to the house, she had been allowed to visit the secret hidden places, he was showing her his treasures and talking about his experiments. She had even been there for "The striking drawers". That was her that arrived thrown into a panic in the living room, because there was blood and he didn't move anymore.

He was her hero, her knight, nothing could happen to him, never.

Sometimes I would let them play with the cards. They would draw the curtains with just the night light switched on, which was projecting stars on the walls. She was winding a scarf round her head and was putting a mysterious air to give a reading: "One day you will be a great explorer and you will go round the world." The

Chariot is his totem, Simon didn't agree. The prince of The Chariot , with his blond curls and his androgynous face , didn't fit in the conqueror profile, Melanie was protesting, he looked like the singer of her favorite pop band. Simon was launching into a ridiculous impersonation of Melanie's idol, singing in an out of tune voice, she burst out laughing. In any case, he could say what he wanted, she wouldn't take down the poster above her bed.

I haven't seen Melanie since the accident. She sent me a very colorful drawing that represents a horse-drawn coach with blue horses, one of whom is winking. The character which is standing in the coach isn't blond haired, he's got untidy dark hair. She has drawn him a rucksack and his hand is holding the string of a red kite that is flying behind him under a big sun, surrounded by seagulls.

I put it on the wall in Simon's bedroom. The night I slept in his bed, this is the first thing I saw upon waking up.

Before going out of the house, I went to take down the drawing, I folded it in four and I slipped it into the pocket of my jacket, near the Tarots.

I can hear the noise of hooves, it is coming from the footpath that is goes down to the beach. I stop, I listen. Now and then I don't hear it any more, they are covered by the breath of the wind and the thickness of the bushes of gorse bushes, they are going away, I start walking again.

I see, coming to me, a rainbow-colored horse-drawn coach launched at full speed, I draw aside to avoid it but I feel a strong arm catching me round my waist and heaving me up inside. The driver wears a big black hat, I can't see his face. I feel his body clasping against mine but no warmth is being given off from him, he does a U-turn and makes for straight to the rim of the cliff.

Suddenly, the field seems to me minuscule, the metal wheels behead the dandelions and draw two big furrows behind them. The noise of hooves is drumming louder and louder, I see the marks white of salt left by the sweat on the horses back. I try to jump out but he tightens his embrace, he crushes my ribs, I can't breathe anymore. At the time of falling over in the void, nothing left is holding me, I turn round to the driver, I catch his arm, my hand only close up on the material of his jacket becomes soft. Some grey dust escapes of it from the cuff and from the collar, it forms like a cloud of microscopic flies around my head, I have the feeling that they come into my nostrils and into my ears, they are sticking to my skin. Just before closing my eyes, I catch sight of the hat that is flying away, there is no one left, I fall down, it is dark.

I am cold, I feel the skin of my stomach under my hands. I am nude, sat on a stool covered in a white sheet, all around the room easels are scattered in front of the big windows of an art college studio. Facing me there is a camera put on a tripod, the dark eye of the lens pointed at me. Behind the camera a young man in black is tilted, his face is half masked with his dark hair but when he straightens up and smiles at me, with a satisfied air, I recognize my son's smile, this is Vincent, Simon's father.

He was only making black and white photos that he was printing in big format. Over them, he was painting, always in black, abstract shapes, until making the initial motif disappear, more often than not nude women in lascivious poses. I found his work fascinating.

One day, he suggested that I sit for him. I could hardly believe that a man like him could look at me, with my five feet four inches tall, my kilo too many and my shapeless pullovers. I hesitate to accept. He eventually convinced me saying that, in the end, with the paint over, nobody could see anything. I became his model, he told me that there won't be others anymore, that he couldn't leave without me. We moved in together.

Once or twice I happened to pass a girl on the stairs. I remembered having seen her at college. I came into the flat furious. He was there, quiet, slouched on the settee, a cigarette on his lips. "You are already back?"

I threw out his things through the window, he didn't understand. Monique came to ask him advice about black and white developing techniques.

I went out slamming the door and I pretended to be dead for a few days. One week later, I found in my portfolio a photo of myself, without paint, with a few words written on. I called him back.

At the end of our studies, we went away, with rucksacks. He had sold photos, I had a little money, nothing held us back in Paris.

First there were the planes, then the trains, then the back of the trucks, among the sheep. Near St Jacques of Compostelle, we continued walking. When we had to cross the sea, we embarked on a cargo ship in Lisbon. Vincent took photos of the sailors, I tried to write. In stormy weather, I would go outside on the deck and held on to the ship's rail. I was sick counting the hours which separated us from the next harbor.

In Genes, there was Serena, who wanted to become model, she loved being in the limelight.

In Sienna, there was Teresa, who was studying photography in Prague, she wanted to learn French.

In Naples, there was Florence, a French girl who had put her tent next to ours. She wasn't strong enough to drive in the pegs.

I refused to take the boat to Capri. Six months later, we ended up in a vacation center in Sicily, hired as photographers for tourist lacking keepsakes. One evening, coming back to our hut, I found Vincent in the arms of Paloma, a flight attendant. He negotiated the tickets for the return journey. I took my things and I came back to France.

I've never told this story to Simon. He knew the name of his father and that he was a photographer, who was travelling round the world. When he began going to school, he started asking questions, he would tell his school friends that his father was a secret agent and that he wasn't allowed to say anything. For a few years, he didn't talk about it anymore. He had decided to find me a new boyfriend. He would have like to have a little brother.

I don't feel my body anymore but in fragment. I let myself getting bogged down in pictures, until my foot strikes a stone, which makes me stumbling and brings me back for a few seconds to reality.

In the other day, in pharmacy, I smelled Vincent's perfume. I turned round, a man in black was smiling at me. He was blond haired and was wearing glasses, I smile back at him and I went outside.

I often try to imagine Vincent's face today, what he has become since last time. Somewhere, he maybe going on taking photos of nude women. At the beginning, I was leafing through the magazines to see if I could find some photo of him, or an article. I've never found anything.

In a box, in the attic, there are a few letters and yellowed photos. I had kept them for Simon, for later. A few days after the accident, I went upstairs to take them. Spreading the pictures over the table, I realized that one was missing. I found it in the drawer of his bedside table, under Melanie's letters. It was the only photo of me with his father, taken on a beach in Italy. The wind had turned our bathrobes into big white wings, we were looking at the sky laughing. Vincent held my hand, in the other one he held the string of a kite.

When I came back to France, I was expecting Simon.

VI

I am a point, seen from the sky, a little black point that is moving on, lost in the middle of the field, an ant without wings, Simon pulled them out to test my resistance. He spends hours examining us, equipped with his magnifying glass and with a notebook in which he is taking notes. In a few minutes, he will take my legs from me one by one and I will probably end up grilled in a ray of sunshine whose warmth will be increased tenfold by the lens, positioned right in the axis, a few millimeters from my back. Then he will try to eat me the way he has seen the Amazonian Indians doing in a television report, but he will immediately spit me out on the grass before running to the house to take his afternoon snack, which remained on the kitchen table.

I have gone back to my human shape with features of a blond haired young man surrounded with two women, my card bears number VI; before going to discover the world, The Chariot had to find his way of life. I am the man of The Lovers who is not sure, one foot in the past, one hand in the future, above my head a big white sun, in front of it, an angel armed with a bow stands out, his arrow is pointed at me.

When I came back to France, I was expecting Simon, he was there, I kept him. Vincent would understand, Vincent would be happy.

I wrote to him. A few days later he called me, we met each other in a café. He was late, he was coming from an appointment in a gallery, his last series of photos would be exhibited, these of our trip. He kissed me on my forehead and told me I was looking fine, when he leaned over to me, I smelled a woman's perfume with a very sweetened smell mixed with his one. I smiled. He asked me if I didn't mind if he will also showed the photograph he had done of me because Tatiana, the gallery manager, was finding them very interesting. Then he lit a cigarette and looked at me for a moment saying nothing. I explained why I wanted to see him, he stopped smiling.

He didn't understand my decision, found me totally thoughtless and wasn't even sure he was the father of this child who wasn't one yet, it was still time to change my mind. He couldn't be the father, not now, maybe never. Besides, it was me that had gone away, I just had to assume my decision. He had suffered a lot because of this split but thank goodness, coming back to Paris, he had met Tatiana, a wonderful woman who was known to recognize his talent, which I had never been able to.

It was very warm, the smell of cigarette made me sick, I had eaten nothing since the morning. The opaline lampshades of the Art Deco wall lights began to dance in front of the big mirror, I heard the noise of a glass broken on the tiles and I smelled the rancid smell of the moleskin bench seat, then nothing. A hubbub of voices, some people were speaking in my ear, calling me, but I couldn't see them. I wasn't feeling anything more. I felt good.

When I opened my eyes again, I looked for Vincent, he was no longer there.

I came back home. Vincent has let several messages on the answering machine, his voice softened, his words always say the same thing, he regrets, he didn't want it, he has been afraid, he cries, he shouts, he apologizes again, he wonders if I am there, he asks me to pick up, he asks me to think about that, he offers me some money for the abortion. The answering machine is full, he can't leave anymore messages.

He went, he rang, he drummed his fingers on the door, he shouted my name. The old woman next door has gone out in the hall, he insulted her, she threatened him with calling the cops. He calmed down, apologized, she went back to her flat with her cat meowing against her legs.

He sat down in front of the door, on the doormat, waiting. I sat down on the other side of the door, I could hear his breathing, first very loud, then quieter.

I stayed there, without moving, until I heard the noise of his steps fading on the stairs.

I didn't go back on my decision, I thought he would come back.

He didn't get in touch, neither after the birth nor for the months after, Simon has never known his father.

I haven't known my mother, not enough time to remember her. My father got married again quite quickly to another woman who became my second mother. I thought that for Simon, it would be the same, that one day I will meet another man, it should happen, at the right time.

A few months ago, I met Nicolas, it was Simon who met him first.

A gust of wind had carried along the kite while he was playing on the rim of the cliff. The diamond was gone to crash on the rocks below...on Nicolas' head who was fishing there. Simon brought him back home, they have talked during the return, I saw them coming hand in hand. Nicolas stayed a little, he repaired the kite , I invited him for dinner and we spent a long time speaking in front of the fire, late in the night, after Simon had gone to bed, then he went back to his home. Then, he came several times, he stayed sleeping. He was divorced but didn't have a child, his wife didn't want to have one. After many years in Paris, he was came to live at the seaside to be quiet. For the moment, he lived in a hotel waiting to find a house a bit like ours.

He came more often, he left a few things, I made room in my drawers, I gave him the house key, then there was the accident.

Nicolas was away, he has due to come back the day after. On arrival he came to my home but I was still in hospital, he had lost his key. He left a note to tell that he would go back later. When he came, I didn't open. I had closed the shutters and stayed in the dark, without moving, without answering his calls, he ended up going away.

He learned the news in the village café and he called me, he let several messages, I didn't pick them up, I couldn't speak.

After a few days, I wrote to him, I needed some time, I didn't want to see anyone. He answered that he understood, that he was there, that I could call him at any time, whenever I wanted.

He came often, I heard his car coming and going away, he was putting provisions in front of the door.

Last night again, I found them, with a flower, a cigarette pack, a note scribbled on a piece of paper. I was feeling his presence around the house, watching out for the slightest sign of life. As long as the bags that he leaves disappear, he knows that I am there, I took them away only for that reason.

This morning, I didn't take the bag, I let it in front of the door. A short while ago, on leaving, I let the door open, the wind rushed inside. I closed my eyes and I began to walk to the rim of the cliff.

V

Simon is drawing a character in a red coat with a funny hat covered in precious stones. What he especially likes about The Pope, is his stick, which looks like a television aerial. He can probably pick up all the satellite channels without satellite dish. He doesn't have to open his mouth to pass on his knowledge, it works by telepathy.

He knows the cards by heart and recreates them his own way, the details which he likes become more important.

I drew only faces, always faces close-up, characters a little androgynous. Simon found old drawings, he has stuck another sheet below with Scotchtape to draw the bodies, a collection of freaks has been strung together on the wall.

We exchanged the heads to see, we took them down to put up photos instead. I had a mermaid body, Melanie the one of a princess. On his drawing of The Pope, he stuck a photo of Armand.

Simon doesn't know Armand, he died fifteen years ago, I told him his story: the drawing lessons, the macro cosmos, the micro cosmos, the perfection of shapes in nature, stroke, gesture, shade and light. We were drawing very little, we were talking.

One day he showed me the cards, I had never seen Tarot cards, the ones I knew were different. Every week I would choose a Major Arcana, he would ask me what I saw. It wasn't about past but present.

He would talk to me about symbolic value, distribution of colors, graphic composition, characters' attitude, different thickness of strokes, letter shapes and infinity of details which each Arcana involves.

Armand's game was very old, when I came for my last lesson, he gave it to me. Since, there has been a lot of others, I went back to this one.

Let go power, cards say what you want to make them say. I always had them with me. From time to time someone would ask me to give a reading. I would cast my eyes over pictures and I would talk, I would pass on what came trying to keep my distance, to direct towards tracks instead of forcing one point of view. I would come into their world for a moment, I would accompany them for a few steps. I watched the consultant eye, suspicion, anxiety, silence to test my competence, obsession, charm, everything passed in the eyes, in the smile, in the gesture. I discovered ascendancy and influence, feeling the need to know at all costs what will happen, without taking time to live the moment. Nothing will happen, it's already there, the ten first Major Arcana backwards, the earthly world backwards.

The wheel of Fortune raced out of control projecting her animals in space, The hermit's coat got caught in her spokes, trying to get free, he spilled the oil of his lantern in a pan of Justice scales, destabilized she cut with her sword the reins of The Chariot who overturned launching the prince to the sun where he knocked on The Lovers angel, the bow's arrow went off itself, it brushed against the trio's heads to go driving in The Pope's hat, who fell down bloody on his frightened disciples, the aerial was broken, communication was cut off.

I stopped giving the reading, I had put the cards away.

A few months after we moved into the blue house, Simon came one afternoon holding my Tarots in his hands, he had found them in a box, in the middle of the photo albums. He came to sit near me, we spread them over the floor together, in front of the fire place.

He looked at them one by one telling me what each drawing represented to him. He turned over the ones he didn't like and kept on one side his favorites.

His interpretation was really free, inspired quite a lot by his comics or cinema heroes.

One night, Josephine came to look after him, he showed her the Tarots. She knew the cards and tried to explain their meaning to him, he listened to her with only half an ear, took the game back and never talked about it with her again.

The day before last night, I went to get the cards which remained in Simon's room. I sat down in front of the fire place and I spread them over the floor.

One by one, I threw the Tarots he liked the least in the fire. I spent a long time looking at those that remained.

In front of each of them a sentence or a word of Simon came back to me, I found in each picture the detail that had made him laugh or frightened again, I couldn't take my eyes off them , I closed my eyes. First there was his smell, the bath soap, the shampoo which doesn't make the eyes sting. I felt the damp hair against my throat, on the crook of my neck, the skin of his warm cheek against my breast, the warmth of his body, small but very dense, nestled against my stomach, all his weight rested on me, cross legged. He begins to be a little heavy but I don't move, I surround him with my arms, I clasp him to my chest and I kiss his hair, I rock him slowly singing softly near his ear. I fall asleep.

I woke up at dawn, alone, on the cold wooden floor, all my body hurt , only the acrid smell of the extinguished fire remained.

A short while ago, on coming out of the house, I put the surviving Tarot cards in my pocket, with Melanie's drawing.

Five, The Pope, I arrived in the middle of my countdown. Each number falls, regularly, fixes to my mind for a few seconds and disappears. I don't stop.

I can't hear the noises of outside anymore, only my heart beat which is banging in my temples and the deafening whistling of the wind that grows. My hand is tense around the urn, I can't feel my fingers anymore; the one which is in my pocket grips the cards, their edge is hurting my flesh. My eyes are still flowing, I feel on my cheeks the cold track of tears. My feet are frozen, they are still walking until the next number, until the end of the field.

IIII

Four, square, hearth, structure, stable construction. Impossible to advance again, the only choice is going round in circles like a dog to find the ideal position for sleeping. Everything is perfect, nothing moves. Number four is putting me in the four corners of an empty room without doors and windows, each corner sends me back to the next one, identical, until finding myself back in the middle of the room. No possibility of action, the empty fullness, as opposed to the full emptiness which lets me move forwards.

The Emperor reigns in the material kingdom. Simon didn't like this king who, in spite of his wealth, had a sad and impenetrable face, implacable self-control of the one who thinks he is supervising everything. Everything is going for the best in the best of the worlds, I own all the wealth but my life doesn't make sense but accumulating for perpetuity. I look forward to the past certainly not to see towards what I could move upwards. My feet are well anchored in the ground, but the sky is white and empty, overrun with the gilt of my scepter and my crown that looks like a helmet.

With Simon, we drew wings on The Emperor shoes, to give him a chance, in the case he changes his mind.

He didn't call me, they all tried to reach me, except him.

Above The Emperor's body, I stuck my father's photo. I escaped from his kingdom, I gave back the medal and the princess crown, I trampled on my diadem, I threw it away on the stinging nettles, I did it for myself.

When Simon was born, he came. He wanted me to come back to live with them, I refused, he didn't understand but he accepted it. He told me he would be there. He would often come to the blue house, they would spend hours on the cliff, both of them, with the kite. He brought him small-scale models of racing cars, he switched off his mobile phone for a few days and he put his crown away in his attaché case.

He knows, he wrote, he won't come now, maybe later. He doesn't want to make his way again backwards, he doesn't want to venture to crack his tempered iron suit of armor. He doesn't want to stop, he accumulates the appointments and the business trips, he meets a lot of interesting people, he creates, he spends, he is hard up, not for a long time. He speaks loudly, he shouts, he eats, he puts on weight, he drinks and when he is drunk, he sleeps. He is waiting.

He called Nicolas, he asked him what the hell he did, why he hadn't broken open my door yet, why he didn't force me to eat, to go outside. Nicolas hung up on him.

He is waiting for me to take down the photos, to put them away in boxes, to empty Simon's room, to burn his things, to give away Barnaby. He is waiting for me to release the string of the kite and to let it fly away beyond the cliff.

I stop, my head is spinning. It happens to me more and more often lately. I feel sickness coming, I lean forward and I spit. I have no more to vomit. Nicolas' bags were piled up on the kitchen table, the food changed color, red turned to green then brown, potatoes sprouted, some white down spots stretched under plastic. I only kept cigarettes.

I take a big breath of fresh air, movement stabilizes, I start to walk again. I am The Fool without number who is going on. The Emperor went mad, he bartered his crown against a kind of eccentric hat with small bells, he took his bindle and left his kingdom. A dog is running after him, he bites a part of his suit but he doesn't even seem to notice it.

Energy that haunts him is his only raison d'etre, he doesn't know towards what his steps are leading him but he is going there.

" You know what, mum? I know that, one day, I'll manage it. I go out from the house walking and, the closer I get to the rim, the more I accelerate, I take a run up and I fly away, I become light, like a seagull."

I don't feel my wings coming through, my feathers have all fallen out, like my hair in the washbowl when I cut it last night, one million black snakes on the white enamel. I filled the pond, they start waving like big brown seaweed, I didn't drain the water. My head seems light to me, I got used to their weight, their presence put my mind at rest, now it doesn't hamper me anymore. I don't need to hide, I became invisible.

III

I couldn't manage to reach this number. I was a little wobbly with one of us, balance with two of us, number three hadn't enough time to find his place.

Simon often asked me when Nicolas will come to live with us. I answered each time that I didn't know, that the house was a little smaller, that we were fine like that.

Nicolas told me he loved me, I didn't answer, I turned over to the wall and I pretended to sleep.

In the eyes of my son, I was the most beautiful woman of the world. The Empress' jewels are too flashy for me, her crown is too heavy, hats don't fit me well.

I fall over and I collapsed, my foot has just hitched a stone, maybe one of the beacons of Simon's flying runway. My knee hurts. For a few seconds I open my eyes, the sun rose, I am dazzled, I immediately close them again. It turns a little, I stay on the ground, I smell earth, the damp grass under my hands. Sea isn't very far anymore, wind is blowing stronger on the rim of the cliff.

I stay there, without moving, I listen to the scream of the seagulls above my head, these of the children who are playing below, on the beach, lost in the roar of the waves on the rocks.

If I open my eyes, Simon will be there, in front of me, he will look at me, a little surprised, the head tilted on his side. "You had your hair cut? You look like a chick. You saw, this time you didn't find me, I have a new hiding place. I was fed up waiting for you to find me, I would like to go to the beach."

I open my eyes, everything is hazy; I wait for the outlines to take shape but there is nothing in front of me but high grass? Blue sky and dandelions. I close them again, I stand up, my knee hurts but I start walking again slowly.

I didn't let go of the urn, it didn't open, Simon's ashes are still there, inside the metal box.

I put my hand in my pocket, my fingers are touching Melanie's drawing and cards, they also are still there.

Among them, The Empress is sitting enthroned, impassive, eyes focused on the horizon, well-rounded and fertile. This is a Juliette ready to infringe all the prohibitions. In the middle of her femininity discovery, she uses and abuses her charms, her creativity is without limits. In the opinion of some people she borders on hysteria. This is a starlet in a bikini, with collagen swollen lips and silicone bust or a high birth young woman a little too well-mannered who is dreaming of going over the wall to go to dance in a discotheque. She would like The Chariot prince to take her with him to travel up and down but her male ideal is The Emperor who is facing her and requires her to fill her reigning Highness obligations. She mellows his rigidity and he uses her ideas to kingdom service.

Stay where you are sweet-heart, on your cardboard rectangle, your eagle protects you. Don't let The Emperor get round you, he has other fish to fry. Take some contraception, it will save you trouble. Don't take this risk, don't forge this link which ties you up and eventually slips out of your hands.

I spoke aloud, the sound of my voice made me jump. I am cold, my hands are smarting, my forehead is frozen, the pain of my knee wakes up, my stomach is tough, it hurts me. A few meters more, I have almost arrived.

" You stay here mum? I can fall asleep, you won't go away?"

No, my love, don't worry, when you will wake up tomorrow morning, I will be there. I will always be there.

II

The Empress listened to my advice, she became nun then The Papess. She decided to write her memoirs and gives young women lots of advice to preserve their chastity.

She grew old, her features hardened a little, there is no track left of her waving blond hair. She is wisdom and inwardness.

Simon doesn't like The Papess, she is cold. She probably prickles, like

Josephine, when she kisses you. But she doesn't kiss, she hides his body under a chasuble and her face under a white mask, she is only the container of her mind. She is living shut away, without family ties, she knows loneliness but doesn't suffer from it. She is sitting on a shape that looks like an egg, from this egg could hatch The Empress, but it won't happen. I took the way backwards, The empress came back to a fetus.

I am walking alone in the middle of the field, but I am not alone, I am pregnant by Nicolas. He doesn't know.

The day of Simon's accident, I went to a medical laboratory taking the result of my pregnancy test. Coming back, I put the envelope on the table, with my keys. I sat down and I lit a cigarette, I puffed at it twice and I ran to the toilets to vomit. I went out for some fresh air, I didn't see that Simon's schoolbag wasn't there.

Among super 8 films, I found a video of Simon last ultra-sound scan. I watched it. I pumped up the volume at the maximum. He was there, curled up, with his big head, sucking his thumb, I listened to the aquatic noise of his heart beat, it resonated through the whole house. When the tape stopped, I took it out of the video recorder and I unwound it on the wooden floor. I went get some scissors and I cut it into pieces which I threw in the fire. The magnetic ribbon melted, was bent, there was impenetrable smoke, it smelt very bad. I coughed, I was sick, I had to open the windows.

The smell stayed a long time in the room. In the fire place, there was only a big shapeless black stone left.

I can't feel him yet but I know that he's here, this minuscule bean which is germinating day by day. He is there, in the small of my stomach that hasn't put on weight. He is developing, quiet, well in the warm, rocked by the rhythm of my steps. On the other side of the skin, there is the cold urn, stuck in my arm. In the urn there are Simon's ashes.

I

  Wind gets up again, I recognize under my feet the short grass and the chalk sheets of the rim of the cliff. I open my eyes.

First I don't see anything, I have the sun in my eyes and the wind is making me cry, a salted taste in the mouth, I am cold.

Little by little, the landscape that I know by heart becomes apparent. Right in front, the light house, below my feet, the ocean roaring, up there in the clear sky, the seagulls let themselves be carried by the draft.

The Juggler with blond curls stand up in front of his table, all choices are offered to him. Field of possibilities is infinite, he just has to choose his way, but maybe his dice are loaded.

I can't go on anymore. I don't move back.

I remove the lid of the urn and I hang it above the void. Ashes scatter and fly away, they are spinning in the sun, light grey cloud which eventually dissolved in the blue of the sky.

I take the cards and Melanie's drawing, I tear them up in small pieces and I release them in the wind. For a few seconds I find myself back in the middle of a flight of multi colored butterflies, they sound like a murmur.

I wait for them to disappear in turns and I take a big breath. My whole body fills up, I shiver. I hear someone shouting my name, mixed with the whistling of the wind, it probably comes from the beach, I don't turn round. I move my leg forward but it stays up, something holds me back, I feel an embrace, arms shut around my chest, warmth from another body wraps my back. Nicolas is behind me. He clasps me so hard in his arms that I can't move anymore.

Without thinking about it, I put my hand back in my pocket and I find a forgotten card under my fingers. I make it slide outside and I look down to see it. This is arcane XI, Strength.

I watch the sea again and I smile. A red kite is turning in a circle in the sky.

Thanks to Laurent Mauvignier, for saying me I shouldn't stop writing, and for his precious advices.

Thanks to Alison Howell for her friendly corrections in English.

Thanks to all, friends and family who red this story and gave me their feeling about it.

Thanks to Eric, for being my Nicolas.

Made in the USA
Charleston, SC
23 April 2013